How Humans Make Friends

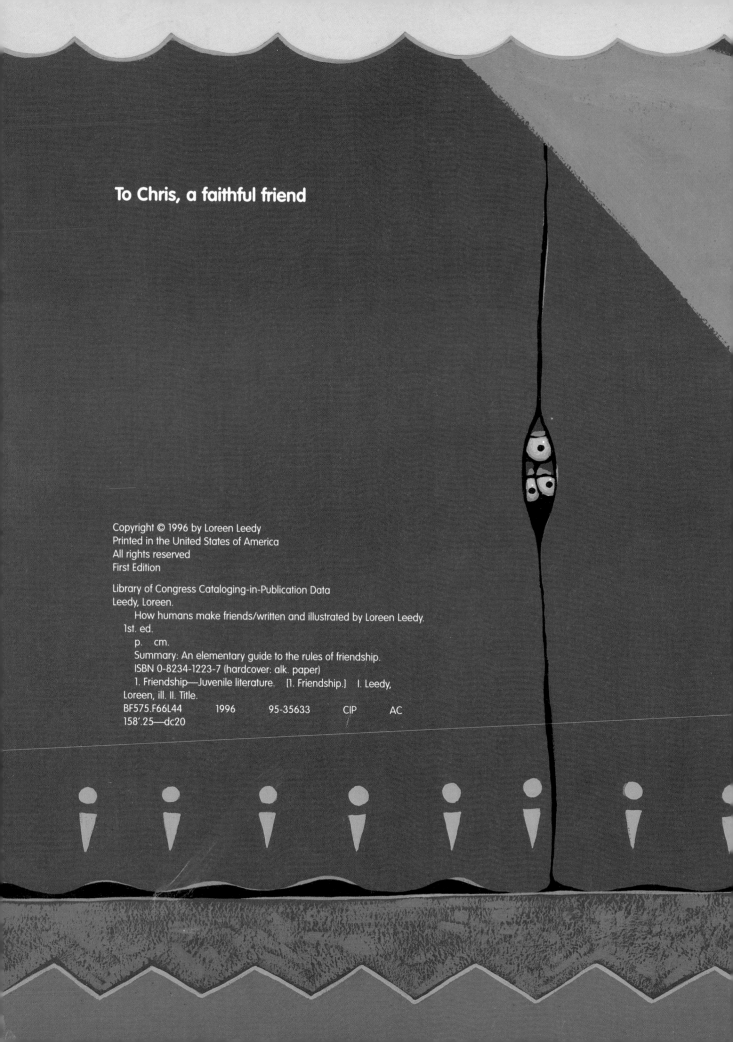

To Chris, a faithful friend

Copyright © 1996 by Loreen Leedy
Printed in the United States of America
All rights reserved
First Edition

Library of Congress Cataloging-in-Publication Data
Leedy, Loreen.
    How humans make friends/written and illustrated by Loreen Leedy.
  1st. ed.
    p.   cm.
    Summary: An elementary guide to the rules of friendship.
    ISBN 0-8234-1223-7 (hardcover: alk. paper)
    1. Friendship—Juvenile literature. [1. Friendship.] I. Leedy,
Loreen, ill. II. Title.
  BF575.F66L44   1996   95-35633   CIP   AC
  158'.25—dc20

How Humans Make Friends

written & illustrated by Loreen Leedy

Holiday House ★ New York

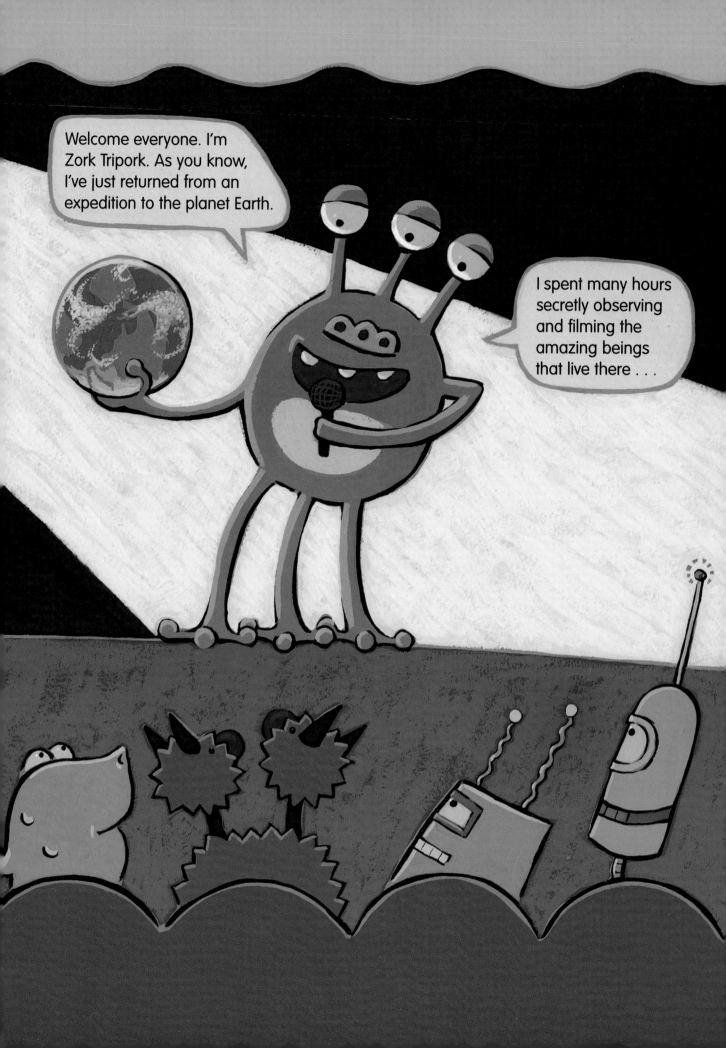

Where Friends Meet

Near Human Dwellings

In the Learning Building

Humans make friends in various places, such as in tiptoe class.

How Friends Meet and Greet

March Outdoors

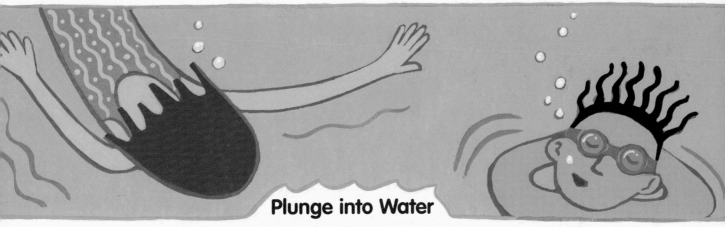

Plunge into Water

Compete at Games

More Things Friends Do

Gaze at Animals

Stare at Moving Images

Create Noise

Roll and Glide

Make Pictures

Climb Large Plants

Hide Behind Objects

Shop for Stuff

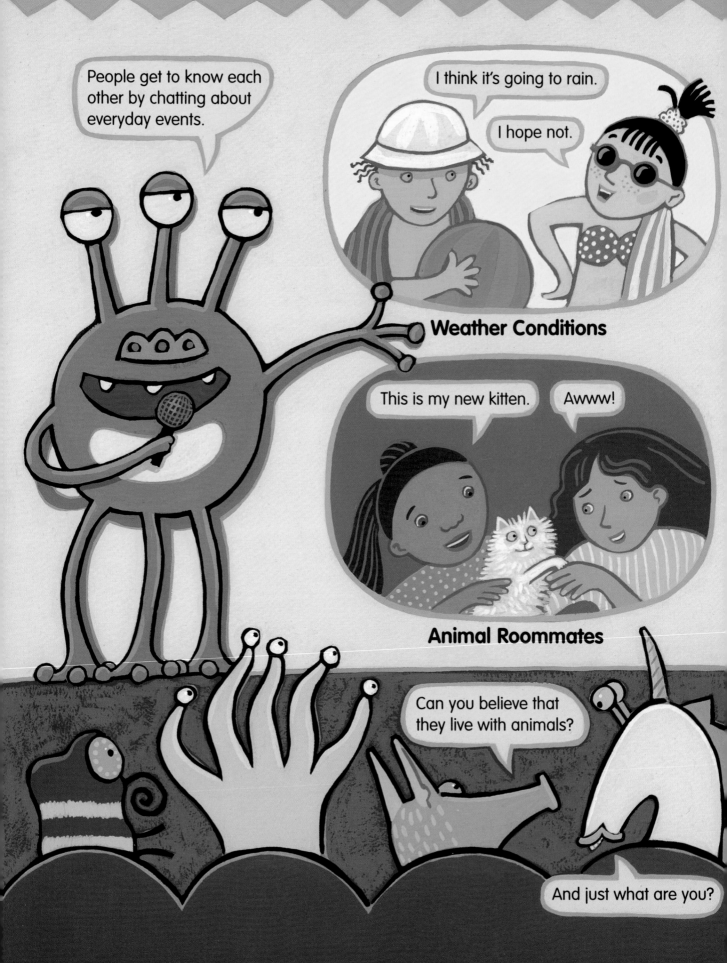

Other Humans

Hobbies

Edible Items

Interesting Sights

How Friends Get Along

In order to stay friends, humans try to treat each other well.

Keep Secrets

Friends can be trusted.

Share

Friends give things to each other.

Listen

Friends pay attention.

Help

Friends lend a hand.

Act Loyal

Friends stick up for each other.

Take Turns

Friends are fair.

Use Good Manners

Friends are polite.

Be Honest

Friends tell the truth.

Keep Promises

Friends do what they say they will.

Good Feelings

Cheerful

Thankful

Thank you!

Giddy

Ha Ha Ha Ha Ha Ha!

How can you tell when friends are getting along?

They have happy feelings.

Why Friends Don't Get Along

Sometimes humans don't treat each other right.

Then their friendships get into trouble.

Blab Secrets

Friends shouldn't tell.

Tease

You're a weirdo!

Friends don't like being insulted.

Act Selfish

Friends shouldn't be greedy.

Act Bossy

Friends don't like being pushed around.

Break Promises

Friends shouldn't let each other down.

Take Without Permission

Friends shouldn't take things without asking.

Act Dishonest

Friends don't like to be lied to.

Be Critical

Friends shouldn't put each other down.

Act Rude

Friends shouldn't forget their manners.

Bad Feelings

Shocked

Hurt

Why is she acting so mean to me?

Disappointed

When humans are treated poorly, they have feelings like these.

You said you would!

Tense

Sad

Mad

Embarrassed

Admitting Mistakes

Types of Friendship

Casual Friends

Hey, I haven't seen you around.

Let's go get some ice cream and catch up.

Close Friends

Can you spend the night tonight?

Again? I'd love to!

Activity Friends

That's one of my skating friends, Ray. This is Louisa from my dance class.

Long-distance Friends

Ha ha!

This is from Pete. He moved to Australia.

Friendships are not all the same. Humans have various kinds.

Keeping in Touch

Letters

Notes

Joe,
Can you
come over
after school?
Sam

Cards

Postcards

E-mail

Telephone

Photographs

People stay in contact with each other in several ways.